This  **Frog** book
belongs to:

....

This paperback edition first published in 2014 by Andersen Press Ltd.

20 Vauxhall Bridge Road, London SW1V 2SA.

First published in Great Britain in 2000 by Andersen Press Ltd.

Published in Australia by Random House Australia Pty.,

20 Alfred Street, Milsons Point, Sydney, NSW 2061.

Copyright © Foundation Max Velthuijs, 2000.

The rights of Max Velthuijs to be identified as the author and illustrator

of this work have been asserted by him in accordance with the

Copyright, Designs and Patents Act, 1988.

Colour separated in Switzerland by Photolitho AG, Zürich.

Printed and bound in China by Foshan Zhaorong Printing Co., Ltd.

10   9   8   7   6   5   4   3   2   1

British Library Cataloguing in Publication Data available.

ISBN 978 1 78344 149 5

Frog

and the
Very Special Day

Max Velthuijs

Andersen Press

Frog was having his breakfast.
"Today is a very special day," he thought excitedly.
Hare had said so yesterday, but why it should be
so special Frog had no idea.

"And what does 'very special' mean?" Frog pondered.
"It must surely be something wonderful!"

He went outside and saw that the sun was shining brightly. There wasn't a cloud in the sky and it was lovely and warm. But that was nothing special. Yesterday had been the same, and the day before yesterday, and the day before that. He decided to go and ask Duck.

"Duck, what kind of day is today?"
"Let me see," said Duck. "Today is Friday. No, wait . . .
it's Wednesday, perhaps. Or maybe Tuesday."
"Is there anything special about it?" asked Frog.
"Not at all," replied Duck. "It's just today."

"Stupid Duck," thought Frog. "She's in a muddle.
She doesn't know anything at all."
Perhaps Pig would know more about it.
Pig always knew about everything.

"Pig, what kind of special day is it today?" asked Frog.
"It's washday," replied Pig. "I have to wash the bed
linen and all my clothes. Shall I wash your swimming
trunks too?"
"No, thank you," said Frog. "But, Pig, is there anything
. . . well, *special* about today?"
"Not that I know of," said Pig.

Frog went back outside, grumbling to himself.
"What special day?" he thought.
"I can't find anything special about it.
What did Hare mean?"

Just then, Rat came by, his rucksack full of shopping.
"Rat," asked Frog, "is today a special day?"
"Absolutely," answered Rat. "Every day is special.
Just look around you and see how beautiful the world
is. The whole of life is special."

Frog was desperate. "But Hare told me that today was a *special* day, a *very* special day. Different from *all* the others!" he shouted.

"I wouldn't know," said Rat calmly. "For me, every day is very special."

"Hare has made a fool of me!" thought Frog angrily. "What a rotten trick. It's not a special day at all and I don't even like it. It's the same as *any* old day." Furious, Frog marched off to find Hare and give him a piece of his mind. How dare his friend make such a fool of him?

But Hare was not at home. Instead there was a note on the door. It said something about a party. Frog couldn't read it very well.

Frog sat down in tears. "Hare has been invited to a party," he wept. "So that's what he meant. And he didn't even ask me to go with him. How very mean."

What kind of party could it be? Surely one with lots of cake and lemonade, and flags everywhere . . .

Frog could just imagine it. Red, yellow and blue
flags . . . and of course there would be singing,
and dancing too.
Oh, how he longed to be there!

Sobbing, Frog returned to his own house.
There, to his astonishment, he saw a flag on the
roof. What could it mean? Had someone been in
his house? Perhaps it was a burglar!

When Frog opened the door, he couldn't believe his eyes. The room was decorated with flags and flowers. On the table were iced cakes and lemonade.

And there were his friends – Duck and Pig
and Rat and Hare. And they were all singing,
"Happy birthday to you! Happy birthday to you . . ."

Frog looked above him. There were flags everywhere –
red, yellow, blue and green, all colours.
It was exactly as he had imagined it would be.

"Congratulations on your birthday, Frog!"
said Hare warmly.
"*My* birthday?" asked Frog in surprise. "I forgot
all about it."
"But we didn't," said Hare.

And then how they celebrated! They sang and they danced, and feasted on cake and lemonade.

Rat played "For he's a jolly good fellow" on his violin and the party went on late into the evening . . .

At last, when everyone had gone home, Frog went happily to bed. "I shall never forget today," he thought.

"Hare was right. It was a very, *very* special day."

Max Velthuijs's twelve beautiful stories about **Frog** and his friends first started to appear twenty five years ago and are now available as paperbacks, e-books and apps.

9781783441440

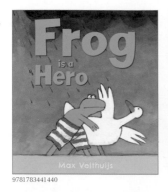

9781783441532

9781783441501

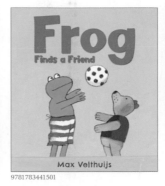

9781783441426

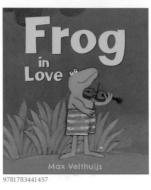

9781783441471

9781783441457

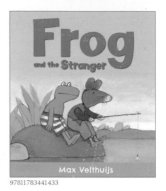

9781783441525

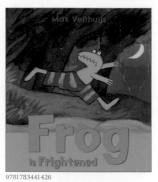

978117834441433

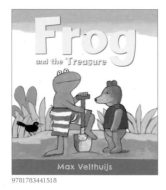

9781783441518

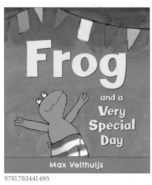

9781783441495

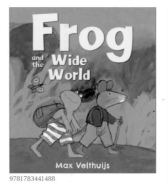

9781783441488

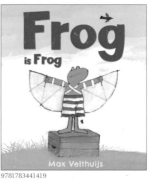

9781783441419

Max Velthuijs (Dutch for Field House) lived in the Netherlands, and received the prestigious Hans Christian Andersen Medal for Illustration. His charming stories capture childhood experiences while offering life lessons to children as young as three, and have been translated into more than forty languages.

'**Frog is an inspired creation — a masterpiece of graphic simplicity.**'
GUARDIAN

'**Miniature morality plays for our age.**' **IBBY**